Inevitable

Poetic defragmentation

WALBERTO DÍAZ

First published by Walberto Diaz on September, 2019

First Printing, 2019

ISBN-13: 978-1-7332406-1-1

Photo: Ismael Tirado
Cover: Gaby Lobato

Dedication

For a long time, I thought that I wasn't able to love, and that was one of my greatest fears, but I was wrong.

To the persons I love, and to the persons that showed me about love,

thank you for showing me the different shades of love.

Index

Chapter I

Autum

Autumn in your hands:
ever-changing and complete.
This is what I am.

Fragments

Here,
my memories,
prisoners for so long.

And today,
words—
It is time.

If these pieces
of broken mirrors
seem like yours,
maybe they were
in the past.

Foolish memory!
If in your hands
or in the soles of your feet
they have rooted,
and a reflection of yesterday,
feed your memory—
they are all yours.

At the end of the day,
it does not matter,
who lived what.
We are all moments,
fragmenting in life
in a fistful of recollections.

Here are my memories.
Do with them as you please.
They no longer belong to me.
Foolish memory!

The Chaos of Life

The day that I met you,
you were in a hurry.
In your hands,
you were holding a pile of pages,
but the wind of October
wanted to play a trick
on you,
and it turned them into comets,
a collection of butterflies.

Your scarf
and your hair—
the tangle of your life.
They all danced
to the symphony of your screams
in despair.

Willingly,
I joined your chaos—
because peace
also needs a distraction—
and by your side,
I rescued some of you,
of your history.

At a distance,
we saw some pages
that had found freedom.

I wished them luck,
and you said goodbye to them
like a parent
that sees their kids leave home
for the first time.

I gave you my condolences,
and in your eyes,
I discovered a real pain.
I was ashamed
of my tactlessness,
but it soon disappeared
when you smiled at me
and thanked me
while you cradled the rescued pages
in your chest.

The day that I met you,
I observed the cold air
that you were inhaling,
your body
trembling of excitement.

My sight caressed your hair,
your lips.
I imagined your aroma,
the texture of your skin.

That Autumn evening,
it was cold:
a perfect excuse for a coffee.
There,
you complained about the partial loss
of your story,
but you were hopeful
that you could rescue it.

You told me
that it was similar to a fairytale
where princesses and princes,
magicians and charlatans lived,
but contrary to those stories,
love did not triumph at the end.

In that occasion,
you did not tell me
about the villains in your story,
and I didn't dare
to tell you
about the demons in mine.

I offered my service
to help you reconstruct
your story,
and maybe,
in the process,
rebuild my own.

When we said goodbye,
I thought about the pages flying,
about the wind,
about changes,
about you.

At a distance, I told you,
"For someone like you;
I dare to completely mess up
the story of my life."
I think that you heard me
in silence,
and you decided
to turn that dream into reality.
The day that I met you.

Tell Me

I know so little about you, and I want to know it
all.

I want to soak
in memories
with you.

I suspect that your humidity
will make me feel good.

That Day in November

That day in November,
it started to rain.
You took my hand,
and we danced in your favorite park.

That day in November,
the witnesses—
if there were any—
got contagious with your happiness
and your iridescence
gifted them their personal rainbow.

That day in November,
I discovered
that you were magic,
illuminated by smiles.
Your presence gave everything sense.

Bravery

If I were a bit braver,
I would give you all the kisses
that I have reserved you.

Consuming Memories

Among cups of coffee,
I learned:
Your lover's music and dancing.
You always eat popcorn in the movie theater
and chocolate taste much better from your lips.
Among drinks:
your favorite songs,
your lack of rhythm,
sorrows, and failed relationships.

Among poems:
mine said to your ears,
made your toes curl,
and each repetition
had a different ending
because these surprises
were the memories of the future.

Life Makes Sense

In your hands,
I feel fortunate,
strong,
invincible,
and secure.

Life is life
for the first time.
Maybe in your hands
I will be
a piece of art,
a weapon,
a home or
a void.

In your hands,
I know
that I will be lost.

Time to Time

Without hurries, nor lies.
Eternal love, not yet.
No stars, nor fights with dragons,
without quixotic promises,
empty decorations for conversations.

In these cold nights,
my bonfire
in the hollow of your belly button.
And you,
whatever you want to be.

Destiny, let's take it calmly.

Stay

Stay,
don't go.
Let's talk about constellations
and about the things
that frighten us,
about mistakes
and success,
about broken sunrises,
in silence,
if you want.
Chaos is also in need of order!

Don't go,
not today.
Let's join your dawn
and my evening,
imperfect twilights.

Please.
Stay.

Effervescence

Aroma and caresses.
A rain meteorite above me.
A collection of most of my fantasies,
effervescent cells,
skin to skin.

At this moment,
time does not exist!
Total eclipse,
here we are.

Illuminating Memories

Leave the window open,
allow the light of this full moon
to come in.

Let us illuminate memories,
in our memory
and in our hearts—
just the way they are.

Don't ask me for darkness.
Not today.

Calm

Symphony,
shyness of time
and spaces,
unexpected restlessness.
In our sight,
wandering shadows
of storms
and fear,
dust of oblivion,
fragmented hail
in a desertic sea:

My calm.

Rebirth

A ray of sunlight,
on your bare skin.
Me, an astronaut
in a suicidal expedition
in the constellation
of your hair.

Between blushes,
you open your mouth
as if to complain,
but you gift me a smile,
a good morning,
kisses...
a good day.

You rock your body
in my arms.
And in silence,
I thank the universe.
I want to rebirth
with you
all of my life.

Marionette

Full of dreams
like a restless child
that ties his shoelaces
for the first time—
That's the way
I tied my heart
to your hands.

And with firm steps
and a naïve security,
I threw myself
into the abysm
to become
a hanging shoe
or a marionette
of love.

You did the same,
I think.

Loving You Is So Easy

My mouth to your fingers;
fingerprints of a thousand caresses.
The dust of other spaces,
wet dirt,
hunger of you.
My desires want you.

My tongue
to the oceans of your skin;
aquatic love,
marine of a thousand ports,
a shipwreck of you,
castaway in you,
in all your tides,
in your harbors.
My desires want you.

My clumsy fingers
kneel before the morning glory
of your hair.

There's no need of crowns,
nor sovereignty.
My past lives praise yours
that are about to be born.
ou deserve it.
My desires want you.

Explorations

We pretend that we are small gods
and we invent new worlds,
hoping to construct one
that belongs only to us.

We learn to love each other
among words
and new caresses,
and with them,
we promise to love each other
in all the stages of our lives.

Arrival

I have protected my heart so much, and then you come along and defeat it with a smile.

Chapter II

Winter

Love presents itself.
I know that winters transform.
Still, I close my eyes.

Welcome

In the room,
your pillow becomes
best friends with mine:
they share dreams and nightmares,
and they take care of each other.

In the restroom,
your indecisive toothbrush
looks for the best place
to settle in.

In the living room,
our books reveal
their outcomes
while they drink coffee
from our favorite mugs.
The T.V. and the sofa,
patiently wait for you.

The walls are painted
a light green,
and to your melodic voice,
they decorate

with candlelights,
flower vases,
lamps,
and they perfume each corner
with your aroma.

The curtains dance.
Us,
in in the kitchen,
feed each other
with kisses.

In this new space,
you are here.
Before,
this place that was
so mine,
and now
is so ours.
I like it.

I Am Home

It's cold, my love.
A little lie—
he's not familiar with this room yet.

Your sleepy arms,
a blanket of summer
to silence my affliction.
They remind me of my favorite gloves
that protected the memories
when I tried to recite bed melodies.

Today, in your ear, love poems.
Are you sleeping?
Are you sleeping, my love?
Are you cold, love?
Are you sleeping?
My cold love.
Love, is your love cold?
Is your cold, cold?
Love, my love is cold!
Love, love my cold, love me.
Cold! Cold! Love!

You open the windows,
overthrow the doors,
and with your hands,
you squeeze the sun,
and with its color,
you paint the night.

I bite your ear,
but I want to devour your life.
And your fingers,
knitting a roof over me knows it,
and the fireplace of your mouth,
and the tile of your feet,
and the dining room of your neck,
the dressed-up heater,
also knows it.

Goodbye winters!
No more winter colds!
Sleep, my love,
my sweet love.

Transformation

Little by little,
I ceased to be
"Me"
and became
"Us."

Now, I say,
"Our home,
our garden,
our dogs."

But truth be told,
I hate this mania
because you still speak
in the
"Me."

Fissures

With time,
our bed started to feel small,
and the routine
began to create a fissure
between us
where we were getting lost,
without realizing it.

I wanted to fix it.
My arms began to link your body
to mine,
hoping to minimize the gap
between us,
hoping to return
to completeness.

I was decided to fight
for our love,
but that Summer,
it came out of your mouth:

"I can't sleep,
I feel that I need air,
the lack of space
makes me uncomfortable,
and it has taken my dreams away."

That day,
our bed started feeling
empty.

Mixed Feelings

With you,
I wanted to grow
and be happy,
but you insist
on making me feel
small.

I made a mistake.

War

We anchored our freedom,
with promises,
understanding,
forgiveness,
love,
our nourishment,
our daily bread.

Now that we have
everything,
we realize
that we made
a mistake.

We docked the wrong harbor.
The load
turned into a burden
and its remains,
into criticism
and complaints.

That storm coming our way
is no longer a surprise.

I Am No Longer in a Hurry to Get Home

You are right:
I am no longer in a hurry
to get home.
It's been a while—
when there's only work,
fake meetings,
and urgent chores.

Always.
Always!
Silent excuses
to evade everything.

No more comments
about your favorite movies—
they are no longer needed.
Your scarce calls,
almost obligatory,
no longer my priorities.

I exclude for necessity,
for survival
because I am fed up
with arguing.

And those silly dreams
with the stars:
All of them inhabitable!
All of them!

Those strolls
during the morning,
in your favorite park,
still in the sole of my feet.

Now,
this bag of broken dreams
and fresh disappointments,
alone
in other's people favorite parks
but not mine,
not mine.

You are right,
I am no longer in a rush
to get home—
not anymore.

Balance

I was asked, "What am I to you?"
I responded, "You are the perfect balance between
a night and a lifetime."
And that's what happened.

Dissipate

You promised me, eternal love.
You promised eternal love.
You promised love.
You promised.
You.

.

Nights

We slept together several nights. And, many, many times you told me that I made your fantasies come true; however, I was not able to be the man of your dreams.

Wreck

We let storms,
nocturnal silences,
the fear of being in the same place
with the same person
invade us.

Let's get out of this wreck,
honest and brave,
without hurting each other,
without any more damage.

I think it's worth
rescuing the good in us
because it exists.

We deserve it.

The Uncertainty of Today, Memories of Yesterday

She hugs me...
It's the end.
I know it!
In shared pain,
words are unnecessary.
Fragile bravery,
mud,
and dreams—
That's what we are.

Inevitable

This inevitable moment
frightens me;
it reminds me so much
of the day I fell in love.
I don't know which one is worse.

Yes,
I fed time with monologues,
I fed monologues with distance,
I fed distance with cold indifferences
and to drink.
I gave them silence,
silence in silence,
in life,
and I did nothing,
absolutely nothing
to mend it.

I take off because
I don't want the little peace
I have inside
me to drown
in a sea of rancor.
It deserves a second chance.

I take off because
one day,
I would like to remember
the positive fragments
of this story
because they do exist!
They deserve an opportunity.

I take off because
I am selfish,
for my well being,
because I want to be born again—
I have died so many times!
And I have the desire to live.
I deserve this opportunity.

Say Something

It's not you, it's me; it's a phrase for cowards, and
you are much more courageous than that.

Tell me:
I'm taking off because
you don't make me happy,
I don't love you anymore,
your presence suffocates me,
it bores me,
it kills me.
I want to fulfill my dreams,
my way,
I want to explore the world,
live other lips,
inhabit different bodies.

I am fed up with your corniness,
your poems,
your food.
I'm taking off because
I want to
and that's all you need to know.

Just tell me something, damn it.
That's the least I deserved.

Destruction

It came out of her lips:
"No one will love you like I do.
You are my sun,
my world,
my life."
She didn't want to accept
that I also wanted to construct
my own universe.

Chapter III

Spring

Unaware of pain,
flowers bloom during springtime
with a broken heart.

Broken Promises

We promised to not let
anything or anyone
come between us.

We both lied.

Red Sky

Your favorite flowers are red,
the same as those ones
that I did not give you.

You blush in red,
like the undertones
of the forgotten message
in your coat's pocket.

My red suspicions
like the lights of the car
that drop you off during dawn,
red like the leaves
that day I met you.

Red lips in search of new beginnings
or red endings.
The wolf's intentions are red,
as well as mine,
at this moment,
they are the same.

Red like the planets
we planned to inhabit,
and red like the shoelaces
of your favorite shoes
dissipating like the smoke
of the cigars that I don't smoke,
red smoke between the eyes.

He is also a product of the fire
and knows about this hell.

Now, It's Me

I know she is cheating on me,
but she denies it
and swears upon all her dead
that it's not true.

Bathed in tears,
she says that I am delirious,
that I am making up lies,
that jealousy
has taken over me.

She tries to convince me,
repeating phrases
that we invented,
only for us,
hoping to reconstruct
our history
with happy moments.

She tries to cradle me
in her chest,
but her presence
bothers me.
She is playing her last card
because at that moment,
she loses control of us.

I know she is cheating on me,
I have known it for some time,
but pride keeps me by her side,
while I perfect
being the unfaithful one.

I Didn't Want to Love

Be quiet.
I want to believe you.
I want you to stop lying.
I want to end this with an embrace.
I want to see you suffer.
I want to swallow your betrayal.
I wish to evade reality.
I want to cease being me.
I want to stop feeling.
Everything is a lie.
Us.
Love.
This painful feeling.
I didn't want to love.
I didn't want to fall.
I didn't want to suffer
like I am at this moment.

Aroma

I know that I have seen you somewhere,
in my mornings of solitude,
in my afternoons of sadness,
in my evenings of oblivion.

I know that you have slept on my chest
and I have dried out your tears.
I am sure that one day it was, us.

I have forgotten who you are
but that aroma of disillusion
that emanates from your skin—
That, I do not forget.

Wheel of Fortune

I thought that I was able
to achieve everything,
and I tried to reach the moon,
but I got distracted by the stars.

I said I would be faithful,
but I lied.
I was eager to live an adventure—
the kind that takes you to the moon
without having to take your feet
off the ground,
and I forgot about your pillow
close to mine,
of your aroma
that I loved so much.

Now,
I am falling,
falling,
and I know that there won't be anyone
to pick up
the broken pieces.

Bridge

He told me,
"At this moment, it's only you and me."
And I wanted to believe him.

I had felt forgotten for such a long time
that he made me remember
what it feels to be the poem,
and I wanted really bad to be written.

Intentionally,
I left open my book of life,
and there,
a new chapter of my life began.

Collector

Her trade,
a collector of encounters,
of time,
and breaths.

It turns me into vapor,
an indistinguishable guest,
almost hers.
One more for the collection
to quench the thirst.

And in the mouth,
suspended particles,
rooted prisoner
for the time that is needed.

Today
we will clear things up!
I know I have the lower hand.
My lack of wings doesn't matter.

To the drift!
Almost,
almost in my totality
because I will never be complete.

At her time,
conditional liberty.
In foreign lands,
as she wishes.
And when she feels like it,
in unknown waters.

Tomorrow,
when the day arrives,
when he comes
with a bouquet of chills, wind, and aridity
and by arrogance
forgets the nocturnal humidity,
your favorite flower,
he is not worthy of my love,
he is not worth it.

Dew, look for me.
I might still be here.

I Can't Take It Any Longer

I tried to love you,
I tried everything,
but I ended up losing myself.

I got fed up with your games of deception.

I put up with it
until I started
to love myself.

Adventure

I am just an adventure in his life,
I know I am,
but nature insists on reuniting us
once more.

I will make the same mistake.
I know I will.

Who Loved More

Don't tell me that I didn't love you
enough like you deserved.
Love is not measured in tears,
in wails,
in threats,
in moans.

Love can be a silent pain.
Love knows when to let go,
even if your soul is screaming
for that person to stay.

Love is when you swallow those words
to not hurt loved ones.

Love is always present,
no matter the distance.

Don't tell me that I didn't love you.
Don't question what I felt for you.
Don't try to drag this feeling on the floor.

Love is not a competition,
where at the end, you get a prize that states,
"I loved the most!"

Each person loves their own way,
I loved you the way I knew,
but in the end,
we each had a different definition
of love.

Don't Blame the Future

Make no mistake,
you don't need to forgive me
about anything.
You were my yesterday— that's it.

Don't try to reconstruct my story
when yours doesn't satisfy you.
Don't try to blame the future of your past.
That's not the way things work.
That's not how they work!

Make no mistake,
I never pretended to be
your charming prince,
the one who would resolve
all of your problems.

I just wanted to be a man
that could help you write
a new life story,
but you insisted on rescuing
your inconclusive past.

Now you realize
that your lies overshadow all the truths.
It's a pity that truth
doesn't have the same effect.

Good Luck

Maybe you are right...
Perhaps you deserve better things,
better people,
a love worthy of you,
someone who loves you
and accepts you, always,
as you are.

Go ahead, love,
go search for your dreams.
Explore the universe.
And never transform into a meteorite
because from here,
you are leaving as a star.

Failure

We promised to love each other in all the stages of
our lives,
but we failed love,
we failed.

Us,
the ones from yesterday,
are no longer the same.
I'd like to think that with time,
we have matured,
and we have learned to recognize
what we desire
and that which makes us happy.

In our beginning,
during that time,
we didn't know what we were promising.
The illusion and the need to go faster than time
blinded us,
but life forced us
to open our eyes.

It wasn't our time yet.
Our forever after
wasn't ready for us yet.

Friends

She told me, "Let's be friends."
I answered, "Of course."
We both lied!
Friendship was the last thing we wanted.

Chapter IV

Summer

Between us: Summers.
The heat was a distraction,
and we both got burned.

Oblivion

I know you are going to hurt me,
but I am ready to cry,
as much as I need to.

I am prepared to leave your memories in the past.

I am ready to stop illuminating my life
with the sparkle in your eyes.
I am ready to forget
that you made me feel and tremble.
I am ready to end
needing your body's warmth
that stills blazes in my lips.
I am ready to try it.
I am ready because
I need to live without you.

I know that with time,
I will forget about you.
I am sure
that I will be successful.

We Deserved More

During your goodbye,
I cried sorrows
like never before.
The fear of loneliness
made its presence,
but I could no longer
handle that farce.

I was sorry that I had left my heart
in the wrong place,
by your side.

The need to feel love blinded me.
I was tired of lying,
I was tired of saying
that nothing was wrong with me
when there was an uncontrollable storm
inside me.
I was tired of giving you caresses
that no longer belonged to you.

And you,
you deserved much more than that,
and so did I.

Just in Case

The door is open just in case.
I hope not,
but it would be much more comfortable.

Moments of cowardice,
I wait without wanting.

It Doesn't Matter Anymore

It's a full moon,
and the open windows hurt me;
they remind me of your open arms,
and I get full of your absence,
of your memories,
and melancholy.

On nights like this one,
we used to make love,
and under its light,
I engraved all of your gestures.

My loneliness misses you,
but it is better that you don't know it.
It's a full moon,
but it doesn't matter,
because you are not here.

I Search for You

I am fed up of searching for you,
of comparing you,
wanting to find you in other people.

I want to get rid of this fucking obsession,
of searching for your aroma,
your kisses,
your warmth,
In other bodies,
in passing moans,
in futile searches
that only intensify your absence.

I need to get this feeling out of me.
I need to forgive you for leaving me,
for not loving me forever
as you promised.

I need to forgive myself
for leaving in other bodies
endless caresses
that still had your name.
I want to end this nightmare.

Storm

I made the best I could
with the flashes of lightning
from your storm
because I thought
that they illuminated
my darkness,
but I was wrong.

Today
I build a paper boat
with your memories,
and I will let it sail
in my twilights
until it sinks
in the horizon,
until I find
the peace
that I need.

My mistake
was to lose myself
for you
when I was trying
to find
myself.

Naked

It rains.
Under the rain, I remain still.
Memories of better times,
all of them, invade me,
all of me.

I need to clean my soul;
it has been such a long time that I haven't.
I need to empty or fill this massive void.

My life trembles,
and I think I will become undone.
I hope I will.
I feel that I am asphyxiating,
but I discover a burst of hope
that stills exist inside me.

The rain erases my thunderstorms,
and with its magic,
it also softens my memories.

The rain is gone,
as well as the weeping
and they leave their petrichor.
The smell of nostalgia: what we used to be.
The aroma of the future: what we will become.

At a Distance

When we loved each other,
I used to caress you slowly,
delicately,
and I used to kiss your body
with frenzy
because you were my whole galaxy.

When we loved each other,
we were a deluge of stars,
and we made our dreams come true
as we pleased.

Today,
you are no longer with me,
but during each full moon,
every cell of my body
tingles gently,
and I think of you,
the same way I did
those days,
when we used to love each other.

Wish Come True

I was happy with you.
I learned how to love,
and I realized
that I also deserved to be loved.
I learned that stars are reachable
when love is real.

I made you the reason for my existence,
and in spite of everything,
it was worth it.

I do not regret meeting you.
I had asked for you,
and that's precisely
what destiny gave me.

Erasing You

It's true,
I missed you,
and without you,
I felt lost.

In my attempts to forget about you,
I shaped my figure in wax,
and I threw it in the fire
so I could liberate myself
from the pain
I felt from you.

I asked all the gods
to help me to pull you out
of my thoughts.

During that time,
I was miserable.
I was air,
but I needed to be wind.
My life had no purpose,
and I had many desires to live.

Remember Me Beautifully

Fall in love again
and make someone else happy
the same way you made me.

Love whoever you want
and don't give any explanations:
love is ineffable,
and it's always worth it.

Share your happiness
and your smile with others;
they go very well on you,
and they are
some of your best weapons.

Do as you please
but don't hurt anyone,
accomplish everything
that you still need to do
and dream,
never stop dreaming.

Live life.
Dance and have lots of fun.
Travel more.
Go out for a stroll.
Enjoy tasty meals
but eat well
and take care.

Don't hold grudges
because I know they affect you.
Try to forgive those
who have wronged you.
Don't let rancor
steal your essence.

Relax a bit more.
Don't take everything so seriously.
Miss work because you want to,
not because it's a necessity.

Listen with more attention.
Forget about your cell
and make eye contact,
like you used to do with

me when you were trying
to win me over.
You have a beautiful gaze,
share it.

Don't watch so much T.V.
Don't exaggerate with the medicine—
sometimes a breath of fresh air
can do you much better.

Cry once in a while,
crying is good,
and it cleans the soul.
Cry like you mean it
because crying is for the brave,
and you are a warrior.

If you can,
beautifully remember me
but try not to forget about me.
If all of a sudden,
you no longer think about me,
don't worry,
I know that I will always live in you
like you do in me.

We carry our story tattooed in our heart,
even if we try to erase it.
Learn from our mistakes,
so you don't make them again.
Don't ever forget that I was happy with you
because you showed me how to love life
and above all,
how to love myself,
with my virtues
and imperfections.

Once in awhile,
surprise my memory:
Eat some fruit,
taste an avocado,
drink a glass of milk,
or eat a cake,
in my honor.
And even though,
I will not be able to respond,
wish me a good day,
at a distance
gift me a kiss,
a hug,
or a goodbye
before oblivion
arrives.

Blots and alterations

Sometimes, I like to think
that you were only a character
of my imagination,
but that's not the way it is.
In my book of life,
you are the main chapter.
You wrote in me
all the emotions that you craved,
that we both desired.
In the process,
there were blots from your part,
and alterations from mine,
we changed stories
and added characters
as we pleased,
as it suited us.

Both of us were good and bad,
we were human.
However,
you are that mistake
that I would make again,
in this life
and all the others
that I still have to live.

Defragments

Here I leave
what used to be memories.
I have carried them
for so long
in my mind.

If any of these moments
seem like yours,
if they have made you remember
what you lived one day,
maybe they used to belong to you.

Perhaps,
without you realizing it
in the path of life,
you fragmented in unknown spaces
and with every step,
you left memories
too heavy to carry.

Today,
I do the same thing:
I leave here,
in oblivion moments and memories—
they are yours.

If at this moment,
you don't recognize them,
maybe tomorrow
they will be part of your story,
of your memories.

Look for yourself,
search for yourself in these memories,
because now,
they belong to you.

About the Author

Walberto Diaz was born in Mexicali Baja California, Mexico. When he was seven years old, his family moved to the United States, and it was in that country where he studied and grew up. Doctor in Education, language professor, writer, poet, and translator. He teaches language, literature, and culture classes. He also develops and teaches online courses for different universities in San Diego, the same city that he calls home.

He started writing since he was a teenager and have published his work in university magazines. In the last two years, he has published his work on Instagram under the name @walbertopoetry. In this same platform, he created @lavozdelaspalabras to offer more visibility to poets and writers.

Social Media

You can follow the author on:
Instagram: @walbertopoetry
twitter: @walbertopoetry
Facebook: @walbertopoetry
webpage: walbertodiaz.com

Books by Walberto Díaz

Nostalgia. Desfragmenatción Poética.
(Spanish Version)

www.ingramcontent.com/pod-product-compliance
Lightning Source LLC
Chambersburg PA
CBHW030458130626
46549CB00007B/2777